STAYING GOLD

A COLLECTION OF SHORT STORIES

EMILY FAULCONER

CONTENTS

COUNTING DEMONS

I SAW HER IN A DREAM. SHE WALKED LIKE SOMEONE who'd never strolled before; she stomped the ground turning glass to sand faster than a hurricane of blades. Tattered gloves covered filthy hands, filthy sleeves covered skinny arms, skinny jeans covered worn legs, and worn boots covered tattered feet. She had a symphony of tired attire, and a determined body.

Her skin was burnt caramel, her hair was a canvas of colors, and her eyes were as dark as alleys on late night escapades through the city. Demons swirled in those eyes as surely as they wandered the plains of my dreams. They taunted, tempted, and tormented with a glance; they asked, "Are you the one I'm dancing with tonight?"

I was never the one to dance with her, but I knew her story — she wore it on her shoulders piled high like paperwork. Her life had started in a bar. Her attachment to her mother was cut with a snapped pool stick. She was raised in an uneven ratio — daddy's little girl, mommy's little bitch. Daddy didn't want to be a little bitch too, so the ratio became a whole number.

She learned her letters and her numbers by buying cigarettes so that mommy could keep praying to the reaper. She fell into that faith. She learned how to live and die at the same time. She started doing odd jobs. She bought books, and she carried those other worlds around with her. Her mommy began to succumb to the reaper, and she stopped working. During the day she cursed mommy, wishing she would die; during the night she slept alone, praying mommy would live. She begged God to send angels before she slept, but in her sleep she was counting demons. Satan listened, and mommy died.

She found new guardians. She traveled new realms of hallucinogenic inquiry with comrades. She found her home on couches and in jail cells. One reality wasn't enough; she had to have many. Those realities ran together. Then multiple realities weren't enough, and she had to have none. The chaos of reality was too much, but the order of fiction was just right. She wanted to walk on starlight and swim through the earth. She settled into the comfort of unconsciousness; she thrives in the philosophy of thoughtlessness.

She parades through my dreams counting demons in her paradise. She sings and she asks, "Who is going to dance with me tonight?" I see her in my nightmares, and I say, "Me."

DRINK

"WHEN WAS YOUR LAST CONFESSION, MY SON?"

"Years," David answered. He turned his face away from the screen. "Not since I was a little boy. I don't usually do this kinda thing." He remembered when his mother would make him go to the confession booth. She'd kneel him down for the prayers, and then kick him in and shut the door. He had hated looking toward the screen. He'd always imagined that if he looked at the screen, he'd see the Father's eyes popping through the little holes to judge him for spilling his brother's chocolate milk.

"What is it you *do* want?" the Father asked.

"I just want to tell my story, all right? Momma told me that if I ever had a problem, I could turn to God for forgiveness. Is that right?"

"Yes, that's right."

"Good." David sucked in his breath as his mind raced to find a good starting point for his story. Precisely when had he screwed up? In retrospect, it seemed as if he'd never actually done *anything* right. Shifting uncomfortably in his seat, he began. "So, my wife left this Sunday. She took Melanie."

"Are you finished with this pitcher, sir?"

David was startled by the peppy voice, a drastic juxta-position to the familiar drone of the Cubs announcer reporting the latest plays on the TV. He turned toward the young man standing over his table. The newbie, a kid David was sure could be no older than his own son, stood nearby with a towel and his nearly drained pitcher of Bud Light in hand. David frowned and shrugged. "Finished with this pitcher, the starting pitcher, and every pitcher the Cubs have tried out this season. How about you?"

The young man looked at David with surprise and even the slightest bit of horror at being asked such a left-field question. A satisfied grin came across David's face. He loved breaking in the newbies. "Call me David. Yeah, I'm finished with the pitcher, and you can tell Mary that I won't be needing another one tonight. Gotta go into the scrapyard early tomorrow." David watched the kid try to give a cool nod before retreating to the bar. When he rose from his seat, he felt just a little taller than usual. It was strange to leave the bar when he could still hear the TV. None of the college kids had shown up yet. Mr. Jim Deshaies continued his breathless string of exclamations uninterrupted on the bar's only TV.

He left as fast as his leg would allow. With how cold it was getting, he knew that any hesitation would result in the metal parts in his knee freezing over. The dopey, neon face of good ol' Friar Tuck soon faded in the thick, Chicago fog. Hazardous though it was, he didn't stop at any crosswalks. The air was too cold, and there wasn't enough alcohol in his system. He was sure that if he stopped walking, he wouldn't be able to keep going, and he'd become West Wellington's very own Tin Man.

When he arrived at his small home, he saw the kitchen light was on, and he was surprised that anyone was awake. Did it really take that long for him to get through his third pitcher on other Sundays? He'd gone on such a long streak in his routine on the previous seven or so Sundays that he'd entirely forgotten what it was like to get home earlier than one in the morning.

He crept through the dark living room and peeked into the kid's room. In one bed under a mound of blankets, he spotted curly blonde hair sticking out at various angles. A smile briefly touched his face as he recognized his little porcupine, Melanie, sleeping soundly as she always did when he checked each Sunday night. David's eyes reluctantly wandered to the other side of the room. Gabe was on his phone playing one of his mindless games. David frowned and opened the door just a little wider -- just enough to make the rusty hinges sound as a warning to Gabe to shut it down for the night, or else. There was an annoyed sigh, the flash of a glare from his bed, and the light was turned off. David shut the door with a grumble. "Who the hell taught that kid attitude? I didn't teach him no attitude."

David continued his survey of the house, turning the corner toward the kitchen. As he entered, he noticed an

energetic burst of movement. Katherine shoved something down her throat, turned around, and punched a
bottle into her purse.

"Katie?"

Katherine slowly moved her purse to her bosom. She
carefully zipped the bag and clenched and unclenched
the handle. Cheap vinyl squeaking under her fingers was
the only sound between them. She took a long-held
breath. "Yes, David?"

"The hell was that?"

"What?"

"What you just took."

Katherine was sly enough to act dumb, but she wasn't
spirited enough to lie directly. Her cherry-pit eyes looked
anywhere but at him. She set the bag down and transi-
tioned to wringing her hands. She was particularly fond
of rubbing her right thumb. "It was medicine, David."

"What for? You sick?"

"Kinda."

"Kinda?"

"Honey, I've told you about this before. My anxiety is
severe —"

"How much did that shit cost? You're telling me you
spent my money on worry medicine? I'm already paying
for you to have a therapist, aren't I?"

"The therapist is to help me figure out what my problems are. She highly suggested the medicine, and it's
really been helping."

"Yeah, it's been helping your therapist. It isn't real,
Katherine, it's bullshit. She's getting money; you're

getting played. You're such a moron sometimes. What do you need help with anyway, huh?"

Katherine winced and turned to look around the kitchen. She moved to the counter and grabbed one of Melanie's sippy cups — a pink one covered in cartoon ponies — and brought it to the sink to wash. "I'm sorry, I just — I'm hurting a lot. There's this overwhelming pressure. Fear—"

"You're hurting? Are you telling me you're in pain, Katherine?" David felt his face get red. What did she know about pain? Did *she* have to go through surgery every other year and still work? Did *she* have to get glared at every time she went out of the house in the day?

"Oh, please don't start this…"

"You don't know fucking shit about *pain*, Katherine."

There were tears burgeoning in her eyes. Secretly, David loved to see those tears. He knew his wife wasn't perfect. It was his job to remind her that sometimes she could be a real bitch to deal with. The tears meant he was winning. He walked over to the sink to get a glass of water, and he made a point of leaning on his bad side. The metal of his prosthetic creaked a bit under his weight. She turned away from him as she wiped at her eyes. "Just because you're in pain doesn't mean I'm not hurting too. For Christ's sake, you have to understand that! Just because you're fucked doesn't mean you know everything!"

David set his glass down. "Jesus Christ, Katie, are you listening to yourself? Why do you hate me so much? Is it because I'm 'fucked?' Do you hate me because I'm so 'fucked?' Why do you stay if you can't stand to be around me, huh?"

Katherine turned toward him quickly. Her mouth twitched between a look of irritation and of guilt. She took a step toward him. "Honey, I don't hate you. I never said that I hate you."

"Do you know how you sound, Katherine? How am I supposed to believe you love me if all you do is take, take, take? Do you even give a shit about my side?"

More tears. She took a shivering breath as she battled to get her words out. "Honey, please, I don't hate you! I *do* give a shit. I'm always trying to think about you; it's just hard when you're away all the time. I'm sorry I'm weak. I'm not perfect. I'm still trying to work through a lot of things with myself, I promise. Babe, I love you."

David frowned. He finished the last of his water. "Fine." He recognized the end of their battle. "I love you too." He was tired. It wasn't about the medicine anymore. It was about her. That was for another night, though; if he'd known they'd be having that argument then he'd have had that third pitcher. Katherine moved forward and hugged him around the middle. He leaned on the counter and wrapped just one arm around her. He sighed and checked the baseball score on his phone, and then spilled the rest of his water into the sink.

The newbie, Cain, brought David's fourth pitcher with a nervous nod of the head. David found himself amused at how quickly the kid darted away. What kind of name was Cain, anyway? It was a punk's name, in his opinion —

the kind of name given to encourage 'uniquity' and to 'challenge the system.' The college crowd had finally filtered their way in and they were crowded around the TV. The Cubs were doing good this year, and so were Friar Tuck's sales. They were all a bunch of hopefuls. David turned his attention to the full pitcher in front of him and he frowned. Did he need that much Bud Light in his system? He'd skipped out on his usual third pitcher the previous week. Before he could finish that thought, a wave of kids stepped through the doors. David groaned. Friar Tuck's was his favorite dive because it was usually empty, but it seemed like he'd have to find a new place. The children had caught wind, and the lack of a competent bouncer left this place too open to eagerly bounding, underage alcoholics. He looked back at his pitcher and poured into his single glass. Yes, he was going to need that fourth one.

Two glasses into the additional pitcher, and he found himself riding a pleasantly surprising buzz. He congratulated himself on his carefully scheduled and rationed alcoholism. Bouncing with the buzz, he took a second look at the youthful bar pests. The guys near the TV were older than the rest, and far more seasoned. They were the guys that he saw more often when he was halfway through his third pitcher. David respected their consistent nature but resented their tendency to out-drone dear old Jim Deshaies.

The newer kids were really grating at his nerves. They all stood around the bar and laughed at one another's boasts of manliness. Each of them carried drinks that were way too strong and expensive for them. David wondered how these kids paid for their revelries. Did they work for their right to chug straight alcohol and crappy mixers? Did their parents know that their kids were going around town in lingerie? Where was the common sense in these idiots? What was *that* kid doing going out in just a tank and shorts? It was fucking October. Who was *this* kid with the greasy hair? How was he even remotely old enough to be there? David stopped his inner rant for a moment to more closely examine this kid. He seemed a bit different from the rest. Baggier clothing, pale skin, a nervous posture. He'd seen that same posture before in his wife. He stood, suddenly spilling the rest of his pitcher across the floor. The room immediately shut the hell up. Gabe looked up at his father. For once his rebellious eyes were seeing God.

"GABRIEL LEWIS KENNEDY!"

There was a baffling solidification of movement. It was like the kids had transformed. What once was a gang of senseless, wannabe porn stars was now an impressive wall of infuriating bravery. Gabriel was being spirited away from the bar by a stringy girl who was a little older than he. David paused and then shoved two varsity athletes aside to reach for his son. His knuckles connected with Gabe's turning face, and the boy was sent sprawling through the door with his buddies. The rest of the mob started grabbing at him, and the strongest hand of them all, Mary's, finally pulled him away from the door and into the bar.

"David! Get it the fuck together!"

"That's my boy! He isn't old enough to be here, Mary, what the hell?!"

"That's the bouncer's job and you know it. Calm the hell down!"

"Just let me go! Fuck!"

She finally let go of his shoulder, and he limped out of the bar to hunt down his son. There was no trace of the boy or girl. David was glad for that fourth pitcher. He trampled down Wellington toward home.

His bull-rush wasn't fast enough. He could hear Katherine's wailing from down the block. By the time he got home Gabe's room was trashed, and Melanie was standing, unsure, in the doorway. Katherine was on her knees near the front door. She still had a cheese-soaked ladle in her hand. The scent of Kraft Mac n' Cheese wafted from the kitchen. The look on Katherine's face was empty. She stared past him toward the door, her brow was furrowed as if in thought even as her heart bubbled forth in a whimper through her lips. David gritted his teeth. "Katherine, I found him at the bar."

She looked towards him and tears came to her eyes. "David, how did this... what did I do?"

"Nothing. Christ, get the hell up." Why was it about her again? Always about her? He didn't have time to baby her. She was so selfish. He hated her.

Melanie had begun to approach them, her lips pouted in confusion. He recognized that expression. She was waiting for her cue; she wasn't yet sure if she should cry or not. He lifted her up into his arms and gently moved some of her wispy hair from her face. "Hey, baby girl," he cooed gently. "Are you okay? Did big brother hurt you?"

She shook her head and quickly summoned her tears.

She sniffled and rubbed at her face. "Where did Gabe go?" she asked him.

David sighed. He was still furious at his son. How hard had he worked so that kid could go to school, have leisure time, and eat and survive comfortably? "I don't know," he replied. "Probably to a friend's house, sweetheart. Don't worry about it."

"Are you going to kill Gabe, Papa?"

Kill? Where'd she even learn that? "Kill him? What? Of course not, who told you that?"

"Gabe said that if I told Papa or Mama about him smelling like you, you'd kill him. I don't want Gabe to die, Papa."

"N-no," David finally stammered in response. "No, Papa isn't gonna kill Gabe. Okay? Gabe's gonna be fine. Papa will forgive him. Okay? Papa will forgive him."

The next Sunday, David was watching the Cubs rerun on the TV. The Cubs were doing well again, but he wasn't getting his hopes up. He knew the minute he started thinking positively would be when everything went downhill. His leg was propped up on the coffee table, and he glanced around his living room. A six-pack of Bud Light sat on the couch cushion next to him. The atmosphere was less energetic, but at least it was quiet. He took a swig of his third bottle. Some of it trickled into his beard, but he quickly wiped it away with a baby wipe. Gabe hadn't come back, but David wasn't about to bring the police into it yet. He was sure the kid didn't have the balls to do anything too drastic.

Katherine was in the kitchen putting away the leftovers. After his fourth bottle, she came into the living room and took a seat on the far side of the couch. They watched the Cubs together for a while. She started rubbing her thumb repeatedly. Deshaies' voice faded away as he watched her in his peripheral vision. She rubbed her thumb, then stopped and pressed her hands into her lap. She'd glance towards him and then quickly away. She'd feign a smile at a play made by the Cubs, then give a practiced laugh at some insurance commercial. Her smile would immediately fade as her battling thoughts would make her forget to keep acting like it was fine. He was amazed at how easy she was to read considering how many masks she wore every day. Finally she lost her own battle, and she stood to go to bed. He turned off the TV. He was sick of not watching it. "What?" he asked her. "I know you want to say something, so be out with it."

She stopped. She sat back down and flattened out the creases in her jeans. "I want to go visit my parents," she revealed.

"Is that all?" He frowned, knowing that couldn't be all.

"I'm taking Gabe with me."

He snorted. He knew the kid didn't have the guts to run away from mommy for too long. "So you found him?"

"Yes…"

"Figures."

She flattened her feet on the floor. He set his beers on the ground. "How long?"

She sighed and she looked up, towards him. "David, do you really care?"

"Of course I do, what do you even mean by that?"

"It's just that, I wouldn't want to start a fight. I don't really want to say…"

"Well, isn't that just too bad. I'm not going to play your games, Katherine. Just tell me."

She flinched and started to rub her thumb again. "My therapist said that I needed some time apart. She says that you're showing emotionally abusive tendencies, and that it'd help to gain perspective."

"What a load of crap." David turned away from her in shock. He felt like he'd just been punched in the gut.

"Look, I don't like it either —"

"This is bullshit, Katherine!" he barked, turning right back into the fray. "What kind of crap have you been talking about me to that bitch? Can't just face up to me, can you? You coward." He stood, sickened to his core. He grabbed the half-empty box of beers and stormed to the kitchen.

"David, I haven't been talking crap! I've just been telling the truth about our conversations!" She followed him. The tone of her voice was disgustingly pitiful. He was all out of pity.

"Why the hell do you hate me so much, Katherine? Why the fuck do you stick around here?"

"I don't hate you, David! I really don't hate you, but if I have problems, I have to say so! I have needs!"

"Yes, you do, don't fucking lie to me! You hate me, but you're too proud and too much of a coward to say so. I'm sick of your pretentious, deceptive bullshit!"

"David, for the love of God, please believe me. This isn't because I hate you, David, it's because I love you, and I'm trying to work through it!"

"Excuses, Katherine. Lies. I'm done. I'm done with this." He took a step toward the door and stepped on a small, plastic sippy cup that had been hiding under the oven. He slipped and let out a roar, falling on the joint of his prosthetic and stub. The pain was immense. He went dizzy for a moment, his vision tunneling on the stupid purple plastic that had been his downfall. He grabbed it and tossed it with all his strength out of the kitchen. It bounced off the kid's door and clattered away. Katherine, eyes wide in shock, rushed forward to help him to his feet. He shoved her away and pulled himself up. That was what he'd been doing all along, right? Back on his feet, a long string of curses preceded his path to the front door. The four beers he'd had that evening was nothing to his ritualistic three pitchers in keeping his leg from tormenting his every move.

"Where are you going?!"

"Out, Katherine. I need to think about this. Settle my goals and where I'm putting my energy. Can't trust fucking anyone in this house."

"You're just going to leave? This is important — You can't just — We have to — David, you're injured!"

"Not that you give a single damn. Yeah, I'm leaving. Watch me." He grabbed his coat, slinging it around him, and then he threw open the door, embracing the flakes of snow that immediately clung to his beard and eyebrows.

"Oh, who's the fucking coward now..." Her voice wasn't aggressive. It was sad. Wilting on the winter wind so that he could barely even hear her. He took a step through the door.

"Bitch." He slammed it shut and left his house key behind.

He stayed away for another week. He spent the night at the different apartments and hovels of his fellow metalworkers. He spent every day drinking and riling up the other welders in the scrapyard, and his coworkers were an appreciative mass to his spirited justifications.

The next Sunday, he wandered through the fog of Chicago looking for a new bar to haunt; a new location for his tradition. He found an older pub on the verge of collapse — his ideal dive. He chose a table in the back with a clear view of the TV. When he sat down, he felt the grain of the table, and found it was hard to get used to. The wood was too soft. The Cubs were winning, and Deshaies' voice was too loud. It smelled very strongly of draft beer, or was that just him? He decided that maybe this wasn't the place after all. He left without buying anything and stumbled out into the fog once more.

He decided to just walk and see where the road would take him. He walked for a while and found himself on Wellington once more. He turned left and headed home. It had been long enough. She'd been left to steam for a while, and he had maybe overreacted in that last fight. He was sure that Katherine thought so too.

When he arrived at the front door, he remembered that he had left his keys. He grumbled and reached for the porchlight. He felt around inside the glass until he found the spare. He opened the door and limped in.

The house was immaculate. Everything was in order.

Everything was spotless. He carefully wandered through the living room. "Katherine? Melanie?" There was no response. The kitchen was just as clean as the living room, and he wondered why it felt so eerie just then. He'd seen the house clean before, but he'd never seen it as clean as it was then. He went to get a glass of water and noticed some glasses were missing. A lot of things were missing. He turned and hurried into his bedroom. Everything that was his was still there; everything that was hers was gone. He slowly leaned against the doorway of his bedroom. She'd left. It was too late for apology. She was gone.

He bounded down the hall to the kids' room next. Melanie was gone, too. All of it. Everything that hadn't been his had vanished without a trace. Everything except for the bottle of wine above the fridge that he'd gotten her for their anniversary. La Granja. Cheap, red wine. He'd gotten it for only $4.99 while getting a box of beers. Katherine hadn't complained. Now he blanched at the sight of it. How could he apologize? How could he find forgiveness? He turned and ran out the door.

David ran a hand through his hair as he gazed down at the wood flooring of the confessional. The story came out faster than he had imagined. The more he talked, the more he considered himself from the Father's eyes. How had he felt so self-important that he'd thought he could just walk out on her and have everything go back to normal when he came home? How had she stuck around with him for so long before?

"I wish I hadn't gone to the bar. I should have come

home earlier. I should have apologized. I should have listened more. Maybe if I came home sooner, I could have caught her and told her how much I regret it all now. What do you think, Father?"

All this while the Father had not said a word, nor had he shifted in his seat. Finally, the kindly voice filtered through. "I think that you have learned your lesson. You have seen your faults and laid yourself before God in search of forgiveness. He sees your penitent soul and forgives."

David nodded his hesitant agreement. He turned his face towards the shade for the first time since he'd entered. Through the holes, he could barely make out a tiny screen. Red and green dots faced each other, and an old thumb flung a small bird at an oblivious pig. David couldn't believe his fucking eyes.

"No," he said quietly. He stood up and opened the door of his side of the booth. "No, He doesn't. No one can forgive me. Not Him, not you, not Katie, not even me. You can't forgive someone just because they want to be forgiven."

David entered his home and walked to the kitchen. He turned off the light, grabbed the bottle of La Granja, and sat down and put the Cubs on. People were cheering, storming the field, and singing songs. *Cubs Win the World Series* was streamlining along the bottom of the screen. He turned the TV off again. He felt as empty as Katherine's eyes the day Gabe left. He was starting to realize that her emptiness was an emptiness of energy. His emptiness was an emptiness of hope. He would always want forgiveness, and in wanting, never achieve the right to be forgiven. It was too late for sorry.

He popped the cork off the wine and brought it to his lips. Red liquid trickled down his chin and stained his beard. The sweet and sour scent of sorrow filled the half-empty apartment he'd once shared with his family. There was no more Melanie to hold, no more Katherine to love, no more Gabe to teach, no more God to fall back to.

All that was left was to drink.

3

PASSING MOMENTS

ON A BENCH WERE SOME PEOPLE: A BOY AND A GIRL. They sat close together, looking at the empty stations, waiting. His hands remained steadily in his lap. Her left hand was in her pocket but her right was out, ready. Just in case. Fingers itching. She smiled.

"So… how was the bus ride here?" she asks, wanting to start a conversation.

He shrugs and smiles kindly to her. "Long," he replies. "How about yours?"

She smiles at the response, no matter how short it is, and laughs at herself. "Well, I was almost late, actually. The bus was coming as I was crossing the street, and I had to sprint to the stop. Good thing the driver was waiting, but phew! I'm not great at running…" She doesn't have a lot of friends. She thinks degrading herself is funny, because if she doesn't laugh at it, then what will she do?

He winces. He keeps staring at the radiator, but it

doesn't warm him. "Yeah, lucky. So, I wanted to talk…"

She gets excited. He's starting a conversation with her. She turns towards him, "All right, what do you want to talk about?"

"My life has been pretty hectic. Between moving and losing my job, I can hardly get through everything these days." He scratches his head. "I feel like I'm not being there for you enough, I just don't have the energy."

She looks at him and speaks with empathy though she continues to smile simply because he's there. "Oh, please don't worry about that. I know how it is. It's okay."

"But really it's not. All this stress that's been building up, I'm kind of a mess."

She stays quiet.

"I just really need to get my life together, I need to figure things out, and starting a relationship while all this is happening -- it wasn't a good idea."

She still smiles until he puts his arm around her. Suddenly she begins to frown. Why did he ask her to meet him at the bus stop?

"You understand, right?"

She always understands; she's the good girlfriend. She looks out for his needs before her own in everything, "Of course, your life is crazy…."

He nods. "I'm glad you understand. I really care about you, you're really an amazing person."

It hits harder. She starts to cry without fully realizing why yet. He sees and hugs her harder. He sees the busses start to come in, and he sighs in relief. "Hey, I need to catch my bus. Walk with me?"

She nods quietly. They walk across the street, and he

stops hesitantly before entering the bus. She looks at him with wide, sad eyes. He smiles at her. "Hey… smile."

She looks at him and only manages a twitch before he turns around. He misses her breathe, "I can't…."

He gets on the bus and drives away. She misses her bus as she sits on the concrete. Her muscles curve up in a smile of sorrow, unable to control their ascent. Her moment has passed, and she missed it. She is most people.

4

SMILING

Why did we decide to go shopping that day? We could have gone to see a movie. We could have walked in the park. We could have gone on a trip and ended up so far away from where we were. But I needed that little chain wallet because my old one was falling apart, and if I didn't have a chained wallet, I'd absolutely lose it. I couldn't keep track of anything that wasn't attached to my pants. Why did I ask you to come with me?

Alice, I should have seen it coming. I should have listened to my gut, I should have pulled you away from the food court. I should have let you know that I didn't like how many people were around, but for once I didn't want my anxieties to get in the way of having a good time with you. Alice, I should have been the one to step in front of you – not the other way around. I was the one who saw him first, after all, or did you see him too? We should have known, with the bag he was carrying and the redness of his eyes, but we were young then. We'd just graduated high school – you were so excited for college, you got a full ride. That day was our first day of summer before the next chapter of our lives. It was supposed to end with Dominoes and dancing – not death.

The first time I encountered death was at my grand-mother's funeral. Like penguins during a storm, everyone was huddled together. The only sound I could hear was my uncle's rough, gravelly voice singing so sweetly I forgot that I was at a funeral. I thought it was beautiful. I didn't really know much about what was happening at the time, only that I was never going to see Grandma again. She was going to sleep underground, and she would never return. At the time, that is what I imagined death would be: being laid in a hole, making all your loved ones cry, and, most importantly, never coming back again. Then my uncle began to sing some Eric Clapton, and I wondered about this thing called "Heaven." Where was it? What was it? Why was she going there? Why wasn't she coming back? So many questions were left unanswered.

Me, the quiet nerd who slept in and read the funnies in the paper; you, the early-riser, the Sunday-dresser, the cross-wearer. Maybe if we had been friends then I could have asked you what Heaven was. We weren't friends, however. Not at first. You were from a group called the "Christians." I just grew up a regular kid. Later on I real-ized that I identified as agnostic and always have. My parents never discussed religion with me in any circum-stance. I learned what *gods* were in the Greek myths I loved to read, but to me they were just stories.

When you were nice enough to sit beside me in lunch

on my first day in a new school, I said nothing. I was a really shy kid; I wasn't really good at interacting with a lot of people at once, and I had overheard you talking to our other classmates about how cool "God" was and how you talked to him every single night. I thought, gee, if you were such good friends with God, who was I to third wheel into that? I never did actually see you hang out with this kid, but then again, I'd always had my face turned down in a book. I guess you can finally hang out with Him now.

Eventually I learned who He was. I learned from you, actually. We were friends; we bonded over a sixth grade school project and our mutual love of sock puppets. Alice, you brought out the boisterous child in me. We spent hours playing foosball and talking about our favorite musicians. I talked about the foreign artists that my mother showed me, and you talked about the Christian rappers and country singers your father had introduced you to. We got to talking about Eric Clapton: one of the English singers I actually liked. You told me about God and Heaven, and I thought it was nice to hear. One night we were side by side, and you asked me to read the Bible. You asked me to read it just so that I could play foosball with you in Heaven when we were both dead. I promised I would, but only because it was so important to you. I never really did. Somehow I was always too focused on the idea that you thought I was going to Hell because I hadn't read it, and I had to prove you wrong. Is it too late to read it now?

Me, face wrenched into a wretched knot of horror. You, staring at me, pale and smiling like a goddess in one of those Renaissance paintings. Oh, Alice, you were always smiling. I could hear all the screams, sirens, and sobs echoing around me like the twisted song of a hundred dying sparrows, and all I could think was, "Will I see you in Heaven?" Does God let good little children who never really knew Him play in His playground? Is this farewell and "Until then," or a "Goodbye forever"?

I could feel your blood. Hot liquid burned my arms and knees. Your pale, gold-framed face surrounded by a rich background of crimson imprinted itself on my memory, with the centerpiece being your ever-smiling face. The soulful, mourning voice of Eric Clapton whispered from the headphones we were just sharing. My ears were still ringing from when you ripped the earphones out of our ears, and from the echo of the gunshots. People rushed around me and pulled you away. They were shouting something I could barely make out. "The shooter is down. Are you shot?! Are you bleeding?" A man hung over you, and he shook his head. A woman came to me and checked to see if I had any injuries. She didn't see any that were skin deep, but then again, wounds of the heart are rarely visible. Crowds of people with blaring phones had to be pushed back from the pools of blood scattered across the tile floor. They were hyenas with gaping jaws, shouting and moaning to each other with saliva dripping down their faces as they tried to get another look. Then they loped away as the police started carrying the shooter off; they'd found new prey to consume.

Oh, Alice, this is me: brought down, bent over, and broken as I stare upon the cold, wet slab that is now you.

The first time I went to a funeral, I thought I understood what death was; but now, at your funeral, my mind is tormented as I wonder: is this the end? Will I see you in that beautiful kingdom you spoke so often about? Will you raise me up so that we can play at least one more game of foosball in the end? Or will I have to carry on? Because let's face it, I don't belong there with you in Heaven. Mute, I stare onward. Alice, your picture is smiling sweetly at your loved ones as we gaze upon your final resting place. Whoever propped it against your grave picked a good one: your senior picture, taken only a few months ago. Were you smiling that way before you stood in between me and the devil who shot you? I think you were. You were smiling so sweetly even then because you knew you were entering the door where peace awaits.

Will I see you there?

5

THE PERSPECTIVE OF A FROG

As I walk down the street toward the point where the sidewalk ends, I can hear a high-pitched hum in the back of my mind. It is screaming in my ear in the pitch of D – no, D flat. Soon enough, it fades away into the battling cries of vehicles passing back and forth to my left. I stop at the end of the sidewalk, right on the curve of the highway as it barrels out of town into the rest of the world. Behind me: trucks, motorbikes, semis, and everything that runs on fire and oil zoom past, making my dress dance in the gusts of wind they produce.

As I look down the street in the direction of what lies beyond this little town, I see a charcoal landscape stretching out through the plains to meet the white horizon. I look the other way and I see my town: a graphite sketch with no defining lines or features. Oblivion surrounds me. Nothing exists other than what I see and what I walk on.

I turn away from the street. Behind me I see that I am

on top of a small bridge. I look over the rail into a name-less creek created by a sourceless drainage pipe. Below me, the creek still dares to contain water despite the oppressing presence of the high-summer heat. I see squirming bodies wriggling for space and for life in the shallow waters. I see an adult frog watching over their struggle for life with the aloof acceptance that can only be present in a creature that does not know anything other than survival. I recognize that frog. Andy named him Wallace. Andy loved going to the end of the sidewalk with me. It was always just me against the rail and him next to me, and we'd talk about any place other than here.

He liked to talk about Italy. First it was Greece, but then he decided that Italy was the better place for our forever home. He'd tell me all these facts about Italy that no one ever needed to know. I'd listen anyway. He'd tell me about how Italy is said to have more masterpieces per square mile than any other country in the world. I'd say that was pretty interesting, and when I took him there it would have one more masterpiece. He'd correct me, and say that it'd have two more.

It's funny. How many times had I imagined myself taking those steps? I can see it so clearly now. If three steps isn't enough, I'll take just one more step – just to be sure that when my fate finally comes driving around the bend, I'll really go flying. It won't be scary. With my eyes closed, it will be like falling back into bed and choosing not to wake up. The only scary thing will be the honk of the horn, but the peaceful silence that follows will make up for it. I hope it makes up for it. It's funny. He didn't want to leave the world yet. He wanted to go to Italy. I was supposed to take him to Italy this year.

Oh, Andy. My boy, my life, my son. Mommy was gonna take you there this year. I know it didn't seem like it. I know how smart you were. Never did I see those baby blues of yours asking me, "Why aren't we there yet?" No. Your eyes danced for me; they said, "Mommy, I know we'll get there someday. I know it's hard. Take your time."

I've thought about his eyes every night. More than anything else, I remember those eyes. There was never a hint of sadness in them, only optimism and joy. I often told him at night before bed, "Honey, God gave you those eyes of yours. You remember that. God gave you those eyes." I saw Him in my baby boy's eyes the night he died. I saw God's compassion when you saw that little frog on that bridge hop onto the street. I saw God's heroism when you chased after the frog, yelling at it to come back. And when you turned to me from the middle of the street with that great big smile on your face, when you turned to me holding the little frog in your small hands, I saw God laughing.

I hear the sound of a semi passing behind me, then a truck. Why am I staying? No one will miss me if I go. The only person who would miss me is gone already. What am I waiting for? I turn toward the street and I feel something cold and slippery land on my hand. I turn back toward the creek and find Wallace staring up at me from my pinky finger.

"Where are you going?"

I look down at the frog, and I have to rub the tears from my eyes just to be sure it's really a frog that I'm looking at.

"You made a promise."

"Promises don't need to be honored when one of the people is dead," I argued.

The little frog cocked its head at me, and its voice was deep and soothing, just like the coolness of its touch. "That isn't true."

"How am I supposed to take him to Italy now? In a coffin?"

"That isn't what that promise was about."

I hesitate with my response. Andy had been watching me watch the cars when he shyly asked me if we could move to Italy. He was always so careful when he asked, as if I hadn't already mentioned a thousand times that I'd take him wherever he wanted. I smiled at him, and I told him again that when it was time, we'd leave this place where the sidewalk ends. We'd hop on a bus and we'd get out of this town and we'd become Italy's two newest masterpieces. He asked me if I promised. Of course I did.

"I promised that we'd live in Italy," I finally reply.

"You promised to live," Wallace repeated.

I flicked the little frog off my hand and took a step further off the end of the sidewalk. What did a frog know?

"Do you know yourself?" the frog asked. "When you see yourself, who do you see?"

I frowned deeply and crossed my arms, as if that would protect me from its mind-piercing gaze. "I see an idiot," I replied. "I see someone who couldn't protect the treasure that was right in front of her. I see a failure."

"Let me tell you what I see. I see a woman. I see her standing at the railing above me with the sun behind her head like a halo, and I see a little boy looking up at her like she's an angel. I see her push her own pain down her throat again and again so that the little boy doesn't ever have to suffer it like she does. I see her telling him everything that he needs to hear to preserve his happiness and his excitement for the future. I see her as his savior, his mentor, his role model. I see her kind heart dripping out of her mouth like sweet honey for him to drink in order to enrich him because he has nothing else to live on. I see her choking on the woes of the world but somehow managing to keep speaking those life-giving words. You are a miracle. You'd see this too if you only had my perspective."

I was crying again. Had the frog's voice changed? I could have sworn for a moment that it wasn't the deep voice from before that was speaking, but a sweet, lilting, familiar voice calling to me instead. I look at the frog, and I gather it in my hands. "Who are you?"

"I am a frog," it replies in earnest.

I look at the street and realize that it has grown completely silent. No cars remain in sight except for a truck, paused in time as if waiting for me to step in front of it, and a bus stalled past where the sidewalk ends with its door open.

"What is this?" I ask.

"This is the end, but it is up to you to choose your next beginning."

I look between the two directions, but I look at myself through the frog's eyes. Who do I want myself to be? I walk past where the sidewalk ends, and in my ears I hear that humming sound return, unbreaking, that D-flat note piercing through the air. As I step onto the bus, I hear the humming stop. I hear one beep, then two beeps in a steady rhythm. *Beep. Beep. Beep.* The bus pulls forward into that white horizon, and I breathe.

6

A TIME TO BE STUPID

SOMETIMES I WONDER IF I WOULD HAVE BEEN BETTER off if I'd just stayed in Japan. Isn't that what people think it's okay to say these days? "Go back to where you came from."? At this point, though, Japan is hardly 'where I came from.' Hell, my strongest memory of 'home' was doing morning exercises in a dirty gym somewhere in the alleys of Kawaguchi. That's not where I came from. Where I came from was sunny streets, plastic trees, burning asphalt – I was twenty minutes from the Hollywood Hills. Where I came from was wide open spaces, baseball fields, huge portions, and diverse peoples. Have you ever seen a 'wide open space' in Tokyo? Yeah, me neither.

No, if I went back to Japan it'd be as a visitor, not a returner. But back I might have to go if America kept blazing down the shit hole it was digging for itself. I sighed again as the live-feed election results updated. The orange walnut was gaining. I glanced up forlornly at the

LGBTQA office's TA – he was trying to dance in a stream of bubbles he had created in an attempt to not completely sink into the sorrow I was finding myself engulfed in.

"Where the hell'd you get that thing? It's fucking amazing," I asked, in an attempt to dig myself out of my sorrow.

"Dollar store. Duh," Felix replied, with a self-satisfied smirk. He refilled the little toy machine that was continuously spitting out a plethora of bubbles and resumed dancing. "Anyways" – he always started his sentences with that word – "how are the results going?"

I slumped back into my pit of despair. "Shitty. Almost over, and still shitty."

I watched as the image of America poised in front of me grew more and more red, as if someone had gouged a hole in it and let it bleed out. How was this happening? It was a nightmare; I couldn't believe my fucking eyes. I'd always been a bit cynical. I'd always had trouble believing in the good character of my fellow human beings, but this was beyond even *my* sordid expectations. Beyond my sour exterior, a little part of me actually believed that the greater population of America was morally decent. Fuck that idea, apparently. People were calling it. The election was nearly done, and so was my ability to cope with my fellow Americans. I shut my computer down, and I put my head in my hands in an attempt to prevent myself from screaming.

It was really late, and Felix was all out of bubble solution. I watched as he sat down. He let the last of the bubbles wash over him and pop into non-existence. His own deliriously cheerful countenance seemed to burst with the last iridescent bubble on his head. I shook my head and looked out the window. I hated this year. I hated everyone. I hated that I hated everything. Why had this election inspired nothing but hatred? Even if that tangerine pudd *hadn't* won, he'd still inspired so many people to hate.

I sat in turmoil over this idea when I saw a large group of people coming down the street through the window. I had to do a double take as it was nearly one in the morning. I could hear voices now, just a murmur. Then, suddenly, someone burst into the office and turned to us. He asked us excitedly, "Do you guys have a mega-phone?? We're starting a protest!" Felix and I were in mutual shock and at first said nothing. Felix then replied awkwardly, "...No."

The student didn't seem disappointed at this and just turned away from us shouting, "Thanks anyway!"

I got up from my seat and hurried to the window now. On the street, running through campus, were hundreds of people. So many people that I could scarcely believe so many would even be awake so late at night. They were there, though, and they were shouting. I'd never felt so relieved by the companionship of my fellow students. They were protesting? I'd never seen anyone protest before ever. I didn't know this many people cared so much about speaking against bigotry. There was hope. I ran out to join them.

We marched through the streets. There were people chanting, people singing, and other people just talking to each other. I was mass-texting everyone I knew and taking pictures. I had to be able to have something to remind myself of this moment when things got bad in the future. I kept getting texts back from my dad. "Don't do anything stupid," he urged. But why not do something stupid for once? This whole country had turned stupid. If joining my fellow outraged youths was stupid, then for once I wanted to be stupid. I needed it to be sane.

I stayed with the crowd. We walked through campus and eventually left it behind for the public streets. Once at the streets, we wandered onward. None of us had a real goal or direction, but damn, it didn't matter so long as we stuck together. We were on a mission to let every hopelessly depressed, mourning person out there know that there was hope in our peers. That there were people outside who cared about them, and together we'd be okay. We were going to get through this.

So maybe I'll stay in America a little bit longer.

7

TOUGH LOVE

DO YOU KNOW HOW LUCKY YOU ARE TO BE IN LOVE? There are so many lonely people in this fucked up little world. So many people never get to have their first kiss, never get to hear the person they adore say, "I love you," never get to have the privilege of having someone be concerned for them or check on them everyday. Do you know how much I would give to be in your shoes right now? Sure, "the grass is greener," but love, dammit. Love is something so terrible and wonderful and beautiful and ugly. The fact that I can appreciate it, here in the dark, cold, and dismal banks of loneliness, while you frolic in the fields and under the sun and then complain that it's making you sneeze – fuck, do you know what that does to a person?

I remember when you first met him. I remember when you told me all about him. You were "struck," and I pitied you because I knew what it felt like to be "struck." He was handsome, kind, attentive, interested. I was happy for you because you needed a little happiness in your life. He could bring you to a level of happiness with a word; it took me ten jokes, a drawing, and a funny story to get you to be even close to that level of happiness. I was happy for you.

You asked me to be friends with him. He was becoming someone that you were spending a lot of time with, and you were never someone to leave anyone behind. You wanted to include me. You wanted me to know the person that you were falling in love with. I got to know him. Sadly, he reminded me a little bit too much of myself. He confessed to me that he loved you. He told me that he told you so, but that you didn't know how to react. I asked you, "Hey, what's up? Isn't this what you wanted?"

You said, "I don't believe him. No one can ever really love me. I'm going to be alone forever."

I shook my head. Sometimes you can be so goddamn stupid. I said, "You can't know that or what the future has in store. How is anyone ever going to love you if you don't give them the chance?"

You said, "But it hurts."

I said, "Yeah, it's love."

I yelled at you for a really long time that night. I felt bad about it, but I know you. You're a bit hard of hearing when it comes to the truth. I knew that if I could just yell loud enough, then you'd be able to hear it by the next morning. And the next morning, you thanked me. I was so happy for you.

A month later, you two were so happy. You tried not to gush *too* much about how wonderful he was, but I could see it in your pictures, feel it from the way you smiled, taste it whenever you said his name. I'd never seen you so happy before. I never thought that you could be that happy. It was beautiful. Why is it that neither of you can ever fucking remember that like I can?

I could see that love, that sweet, fireworks, hallelujah love. Do you know how that made me feel? Is it selfish of me to think that it matters? You. My rock, my tragic hero, my angel, my demon, the one that loves too much and is loved too little. In your essence I could see a happiness that could shake away the dark clouds of my world, because at least one person I cared about was getting the love they deserved.

It's so sick. The one that beheld the beauty of your love must now illuminate the repulsiveness of your egos. I can't take the fighting – the constant fighting. Why is it that I'm always in the middle? Somehow I *am* always in the middle, though, and I promise you it isn't me who walked there. Why is it always up to me to keep you two from ruining that beautiful thing that you created together? Do you know how lucky you are to have found him? Does he know how lucky he is to have found you? I feel like I am the single culmination of all the lonely people in the world, throwing myself against an immovable wall. Each bone-breaking collision between my fists and the wall leaves nothing more than the faintest scratch on its stony surface. I scream and I scream. I've screamed myself hoarse.

Are you even listening?

Please, listen to me.

Please, listen to each other.

Take a step back in time, look at your photos, look into each other's eyes. Take a step back and remember yourselves and remember how beautiful it all was. Take a step back and remember that how much you love him should always outweigh the importance of what you are fighting about. If it doesn't? Well... I guess you weren't so lucky after all.

Tough love.

8

VALUE

We slid from the cool darkness of modern technology into your hand, and we were so new that you had a hard time separating us from each other. Your first thought was, "What the fuck, small change?" You shoved us into your wallet anyway, and we were given the first wrinkles of age, of experience.

It was December, and we didn't stay with you long. Soon it was your niece's fifth birthday. She's a "My Little Pony" girl – she thinks Dora the Explorer seriously needs glasses. You weren't planning on going, but somehow the family pulled you in, so you traded me to a guy with crooked teeth for a Dora plate-set at the dollar store. You shoved it in a plastic bag, tied the ends, and imagined it was a bow.

The crooked-toothed man kept me in his pocket, and my fibers frayed from being in contact with the sweat-infused lining of his pants. I didn't stay with him for very long, either. He took me to his favorite coffee shop. They had a new barista, Mary. Mary didn't know the crooked-toothed man already when he bought his coffee. She wrote "Bart" on his cup, but Bart is not his name. He tipped her anyway. I spent that day with Mary. Face after face peered at me as days passed by. The faces were all blurry, and big, green letters blocked my view of their tired faces. One face was more tired than the rest. More scared. More sorry. Mary turned away to make coffee, and my world was filled with the palm of his hand as he ran away with his coveted treasure. He didn't see the pole coming. I flew, blown about by car wakes, sewer vents, and spring breezes.

A young girl caught me. Her golden hair was tied back in braids tight enough to elongate her forehead. Chocolate smeared on my face as she laughed and looked at her giant guardians for approval. They didn't look down; they never look down. She half jumped, half walked to keep up with their long gaits, and she stared in awe at a bearded man with the voice of an angel. She saw crumpled papers, just like me, gathered at his feet, and she tossed me to join them; a fleeting moment of life shone in the bearded man's eyes, and he played something happier. Spring rains splattered me and my new friends, causing us to lay flat against the velvet lining of the guitar case. He gathered me up, straightened me out, and paper-clipped me to the rest because wallets are expensive. He went out with his friends to listen to other singers who were worse than he was but better at networking, and he drunkenly bemoaned his lack of talent.

Way too many mixed drinks later, and the waitress

was glaring daggers into his callused hands. He slowly shuffled out, leaving me crumpled in a puddle of bitter leftovers. She tore him a new one in her mind, but she took me anyway. I stuck to her hand. We became close. She was a good saver; or rather, she'd been telling her friends about "getting the hell out" for a while and couldn't disappoint her amassed audience. Then she went to Grandma's dinner and said "hell" a few too many times. Grandma reverted her back to a twelve year-old with her authority, and I went into the swear jar.

Grandma never opens the swear jar. She lives by herself in a home the size of a two-bedroom apartment. She keeps old videos and records in all the places other people keep nice furniture. Her carpet is stained sepia, and her drapes are both outrageously colored and almost black and white – that's how everyone will remember them, anyway. She smells like Eau de Laundry Detergent, the smell of loving care and fussiness, and during the summer her sweat makes her couch shinier than her thimble collection. She cooks for her neighbors, and she cooks for her family. She's old, but she has her vitality and she prays to God. Old age is not how she dies. Her family uses the swear jar to pay for donuts for the funeral. The donut delivery girl gets me as a tip.

After work, she buses home, reflecting on mortality. Red leaves stick to the vibrating windows, blocking her view of the drenched streets. She misses her stop theorizing on all the unknown questions of the universe. She is 19. The middle-aged man across the way thinks she must be thinking of current politics by the way that she frowns. He decides that it's the hopelessness in her eyes –

that's what makes him think that. The donut delivery girl reaches the end of the line, and she uses me to pay for the ride back to her missed stop – it's getting too cold to walk.

The bus driver agrees. At the end of his shift, he fumbles with the bag of cash in his machine, and I slip out, falling underneath the seat. He sees me: damp, stained, torn, scratched, crumpled at his feet. He picks me up and without really thinking about it, he shoves me into his pocket. It was one dollar, and at that point, what did he care? He'd been looking for an excuse to leave this gig for years now. He steps out of the bus, clocks out, and drives home to an empty house and three-day-old take-out. He trades me to an awkward teen in order to replace the rotten takeout with a fresh batch.

You open the door to freezing snowflakes and an awkward teen. He hands you the three cheese pizzas for your niece's sixth birthday party while your aunt sets out My Little Pony plates. You give him a crisp twenty and he returns a crumpled mass of dollars and two coins. You glare at him and shut the door in his face. You pocket me: just another crumpled old dollar.

Do you know what I am worth?

9

STAYING GOLD

"NOTHING GOLD CAN STAY." HOW MANY TIMES HAD I repeated that single phrase to myself so far? How many more times would I continue to whisper it? I sighed and watched the warmth of my breath fog the glass just inches from my face. My slender white hand rose and wiped the fog away to reveal the ephemeral tranquility that hung in my mother's suburban neighborhood. The only lights that could be seen were from the street lamps lining the empty street. Everyone's cars were settled in their pristine, paved driveways. The silver Prius that belonged to the quiet bank accountant across the street was the closest to my house – at least, in my view. Then there was the huge yellow hummer that belonged to the basketball player who was a big star at the university. I knew it was late when I could no longer see past the hummer. As the fog was wiped away, I focused again on my reflection staring forlornly back at me. I couldn't see my hair; it blended in with the dark night beckoning outside the window. My skin, however, was as white as the thickening moon, and my eyes were a very light shade of hazel. They were often mistaken to be gold.

I looked at my hand and noticed that the condensation that was gathered on my fingers was burning cold. Would it be too cold outside? The sky was fairly clear, so I didn't think it would rain, but the temperatures were falling quickly and the nights growing longer. It might be too cold to... no. I turned away from the window to look about my organized bedroom. I was sixteen now; too old to be wimping out just because of chilly weather. I had a jacket and gloves. That would be plenty to combat a little weather. I took a second glance about my room, and I finally settled my gaze on the open duffel bag on my bed. My mouth moved silently to words that were more familiar than the Pledge of Allegiance or any radio station-frequenting song. *Nature's first green is gold.* I floated rather than walked to the vanity that sat across from me, and I picked up the pair of glasses sitting there.

I looked into the glass of the spectacles, and I thought I saw my seven-year-old self looking back at me. Her eyes were pouting and filled with disdain. "Daddy, why do I need glasses? I don't want to have glasses."

"Why not?" my father chuckled, sitting across from me in the living room.

I looked down and kicked my feet together for no real reason even though I looked like I was furious at some speck of dust in my soles. "They're stupid."

"Stupid? Daddy wears glasses. Is Daddy stupid?" he asked in his usual gentle tone.

"No," I hesitantly replied, though I knew what question was coming next.

"So why do you think glasses are stupid?"

I knew my father. Even back then I knew the way he thought. I also knew that my answer would be pathetically counterable, although I wouldn't admit it. With a longer hesitation than before, I stopped kicking my feet and answered, "Because all the other kids will make fun of me for them."

"I see." My father nodded his head as if he were a sage about to give me advice that would save my life. He always looked like that; like he was about to give me some amazing piece of advice. He'd always be leaning back, one corner of his mouth would always be raised just half a centimeter higher than the other, and his hazel eyes would crinkle in quiet appreciation of his own wisdom. I can't remember what he said to me then. It was some answer that had something to do with literature. He had been crazy about books, and that craziness had rubbed off on me.

He was a literature professor; at least he had been before he'd gotten fired. Robert Frost was his favorite poet, and when I was little, he'd read Frost poems to me before I went to bed. My favorite poem was *Nothing Gold Can Stay*, and I had a tendency to repeat it whenever I got nervous or scared. I loved it because it was in one of my favorite books, *The Outsiders*. It was the book my dad had read to me after I got my first pair of glasses. He used to call me Ponyboy because of how much I would insist he read it to me again.

Did this stand out too much? I spun around in front of the mirror. My arms were spread out as I spun as if I were dancing in some sort of splendid ball. I found myself frowning at the question. Usually I was asking myself just the opposite. "Is this bright enough? Is this shade of orange enough?" That's what I was usually asking myself. Ever since I moved in with my mother, I'd found my life drained of color. When I lived with my father, there were red curtains and brownish red couches. There were lamps in every corner so you could read anywhere you wanted. Everything about the little apartment we shared was autumn reds and rich, honey gold. When I came to my mother's house, I'd tried to emulate that sweet, succulent life, but the house had a way of drowning out all color. It was eternally cold no matter the season outside. Every wall, piece of furniture, and person within was white-washed. Nothing escaped the oppressive shades of white, gray, and blue. I tried putting up posters at first. Once I bought a can of bright red paint and I painted my whole room with it. My mother hadn't noticed for a whole month, but when she did, I was white-washed all over again.

I also tried to wear brightly colored clothing, but that too was washed over like a drop of watercolor painted over in black. My orange-red sweaters and bright green hats always looked like there was a high-opacity mist floating around them. Nothing ever 'popped' like it did in dad's house.

Tonight was different than those days, though. Tonight I didn't want to stand out at all. Tonight I wanted to blend in with the shadows of the street outside. Tonight I wanted to be an apparition that would never catch anyone's eye so that I would never be dragged back because of anyone's intrinsic need to 'save' me. I hardly recognized myself in the mirror. A dark sweatshirt that was too baggy for my malnourished, stick-like figure hung off my form. I had cut holes for my thumbs in the fabric; I did this for all of my clothing. I only ever wore long-sleeved shirts these days, even when the scalding, summer sun baked my arms and made them sting and itch. Underneath the dark hood of the sweatshirt, my left eye judged my appearance with scrutiny while my right eye hid beneath a layer of wavy black hair. Slowly I moved those bangs out of my face to reveal the ugly, black and brown bruise that had been screaming at me all night. My poetic chanting continued. *Her hardest hue to hold…* I was brought back to that same question that had plagued my thoughts for years. Had she hesitated? I could almost hear the voices darting back and forth. They were whispers now, but back then I might as well have been listening to the roars of battling lions.

"You still don't believe me?"

"Of course I believe you, Curtis. You don't have the balls to to do anything so risky."

"Then why?"

"Why, Curt? Why? Maybe because if you had touched that little bitch's perky rack and given her what she wanted, you wouldn't be the broke, unemployed loser you are now! Maybe if you grew a pair and hadn't gotten overpowered by three conspiring skanks, I wouldn't be stuck with your garbage reputation!"

"Jenna, keep your voice down, please. Anne is upstairs-"

"Don't change the damned subject!"

I huddled next to the door, holding my knees to my mouth so I wouldn't make any noise as I cried. Their shadows moved in the light that shined from underneath the bedroom door. I'd had a nightmare, and I'd been seeking out my parents' bed so that their presence could scare the nasty dream away. My lips moved rapidly against the skin of my knees as I watched those shadows dance. "Nature's first green is gold," I began quietly, as I was forced to wonder what 'bitch' and 'skank' meant, and why Momma was screaming.

"This is because I lost my job? Jen, did I ever mean anything to you?!"

"Maybe you did before you became old and boring as hell!"

"And what about Anne?"

"What about her?"

There was a long silence, and I wondered if finally the screaming was over. Then his voice came again and it was defeated. I had never heard my dad sound so sad before; not even when he explained to me that some girls lied about him at his work so he couldn't work there anymore. "Fine. You don't want me here and that's just fine. Just promise me one thing," he muttered, so low I could barely discern what was being said.

"What?" my mother replied shortly.

"You can have the house, the money, the furniture, everything that we own as long as you give me enough to get started somewhere else and you let me have custody of Anne."

My eyes widened as my lips soundlessly continued their chant. I had gotten to the last line by then. At the end of 'Anne,' I was mouthing 'nothing gold can stay,' and just as I felt the line leave my lips, I heard my mother say, "Fine."

It was only a few seconds, but I'd never been able to decide if those few seconds had been a hesitation. How long did a pause have to be in order to turn into a hesitation? How quickly did that request process in my mother's mind? Was there ever a moment when my mom had wanted me to stay in her life?

How long did I hesitate before I finally picked Cheetos over Doritos? Ten, maybe twenty seconds, I thought, as I tossed the unopened bag into the duffel. Was that a hesitation or a pause? What was the difference? I began to load snack after snack into the duffel bag before me. I'd been hiding them under the bed for weeks. I knew that some of the snackfoods were stale, but they were food, and they were all I had. Then came the clothes. All I could fit into the duffel bag were three outfits, so I chose the three warmest ones and stuffed them over the snacks. I walked back to the vanity and slowly took a seat. It was 4:30. I was supposed to call John at five, and I looked at myself in the mirror mentally going over the list in my head that I had obsessed over for weeks. Stash food, pack the food and some clothes, wear something dull, cut your hair, and steal the pills. I was frozen looking at the shining, silver scissors sitting in front of me. They were my school scissors, but I'd taken them out of my backpack years ago. They would serve a much different purpose now. I reached for the scissors slowly as if I had gotten trapped in a slow-motion camera reel. The cold metal pressed against my palm and stuck there as my sweat acted as an adhesive. The metal was familiar, but it did not give me the comfort it had given me before. Now I dreaded its foul purpose as I held it between the mirror and myself. Just a few snips; that's all it would take. God dammit, why was this so hard? I stared at myself for a long while, and I mourned for my long, wavy black hair. Second guesses raced through my mind and taunted me. I had spent so long building myself up to this decision, and suddenly I found myself confronted with that terrible question: what if I was wrong? My free hand carefully moved back my black bangs so that I could gaze upon that bruise once again. I still couldn't remember the blow itself. I couldn't remember if I'd fallen over or if I'd hit back, but as I looked at that ugly bruise now, my eyes hardened in determination. *Her early leaf's a flower, but only so an hour.* Snip. Hair cascaded to the floor like the molted feathers of a forlorn, tap-tapping raven.

I had just turned fifteen when my dad died. He'd been battling Chronic Obstructive Pulmonary Disease for a while. I helped him whenever I could, but we just didn't have enough money to pay for the treatment he needed, and he was in hospice just a month after we celebrated my birthday. He gave me a gold-leafed copy of *The Poetry of Robert Frost*. It was the first thing I packed earlier this evening. The day before he died, I'd been sitting by his side on a Saturday reading *The Outsiders* aloud to him like he had done for me when I was younger. He couldn't read aloud anymore; the machines that were helping his failing lungs stay afloat wouldn't allow it. He told me that I would be staying with my mother until I was old enough to get my own place to stay. I felt betrayed. How could he leave me alone with her? How could he leave me alone at all? He didn't have the time to answer these questions for me as he died the next morning. The last words I said to him were, "I hate you." He'd only smiled and croaked, "Stay golden."

Mother had tried to be pleasant at first. She smiled at me and called me Annie. She even insisted that we eat dinner together. Despite this, I knew she was just putting on airs. It was the same smile she wore for her clients: polite, carefully constructed, and deceitfully friendly. This was the face she used when she had clients over for a meeting, and this was the face she had been using as she asked me to pass the salt.

It was both a curse and a blessing when she stopped going through that pretense. The "How do you do's" turned into "Are you really going to go to school like that?" She went from "Your hair looks very neat" to "It figures your father turned you into such a slob."

She stopped making me go to dinner with her after the second week. She started forbidding me coming downstairs after eight after a couple months had passed. It wasn't hard for me to figure out why: I'd gone downstairs more than enough mornings only to find a strange man drinking coffee half-naked in the kitchen. I stopped eating breakfast after the third time. I didn't like the way they ate me up with their eyes.

Usually Mother didn't really bother looking into my life. I might as well have been a cat, or even a little mouse. The only time we'd talk would be in passing or when I'd have to come down and make myself something to eat, and those conversations were almost always a one-ended criticism of my appearance if only because she didn't know me well enough to criticize my personality. I tried to keep it that way.

One afternoon I'd come down to make myself a sandwich for lunch and she was waiting for me by the fridge.

"What the fuck are you wearing?" she whined.

"Just a sweater."

"It's a piece of shit. Throw it out."

"But Dad gave it to-"

"Listen, sweety, Mommy's boss is coming to dinner today and you're coming down and joining us. I won't have you ruining my life by wearing some fugly outfit I didn't buy you. All right? Wear one of the dresses."

"I don't like the dresses."

"I don't care if you don't like them, you're going to wear one. No daughter of mine is going to be seen dressing so hideously in front of my employers."

"You have no daughter at all!"

Stars.

She moved so fast for someone so frail-looking. Later on I imagined that her hands must have been covered in make up during dinner because there was no way her hand had not been bruised by my cheek bone earlier. After that day, I really wasn't her daughter anymore. I was her ragdoll, and she was a four-year-old girl who threw her doll across the room whenever she had a tantrum. I'd only been in her home for five months.

A year later, I knew exactly where to step to avoid making the stairs creak too loud. To the far right, then to the middle, then the far left. I carried my duffel bag in front of me like a shield as I slithered down those steps. I left the bag by the door and continued towards the largest room in the house. I creaked the door slowly open. There she was sprawled in bed. That night I was thankful she was so loose with her relationships. The newest guy sharing her bed was a living motor engine, and I only had to time the door with one of his mighty roars. I wrinkled my nose as I was attacked by the aroma of sex and Febreeze. I didn't waste time in the darkened room, and I slipped into her personal bathroom and turned on the light. In front of me was a shrine of medications, vitamins, and beauty products. As I gazed at the wall of chemicals, I continued to mutter to myself. *Then leaf subsides to leaf. So Eden sank to grief.* Aha – Adderall. I wondered how much this bottle had costed her. Forty, fifty dollars? My face crumpled into a scowl.

I remember when I first began to wonder if there was something wrong with me. About a year after I'd been living with her, it was like all the color had been sucked out of life. It was like words were no longer magic, and all my books were locked away from me. After my fifth cut, I went to my school counselor. She was compassionate, and she kindly notified me that it would be best if I saw a professional. I went to my mother the next day when she was having breakfast, and I shyly showed her the scars. I told her I'd talked to a counselor, and that I wanted to see a psychologist and maybe get antidepressants. For once I revealed to her my feelings, if only because I was scared, and I couldn't see another way out. The white was murdering me; I wanted to live in color again. When I spoke to her, she was taking her Adderall pills for the day, emptying yet another bottle with her morning coffee.

"Stop being such a baby," she told me. "Depression isn't a real disease. You just need to get over it." I could only move my lips wordlessly as she turned toward me and shut her medicine cabinet with a careless slam. "Besides, seeing anyone and getting you pills will be so expensive. Are you going to pay for that? If you're so lonely, why don't you just lose a few pounds and get some friends?"

I stuffed the full pill bottle into my pocket. I stepped back into the dark of the room and I whispered to her through the dark, "Don't worry, Mom, you won't be 'paying' for me anymore." I turned, feeling disgusted, and returned to the door. The front door slid open easily and without a sound as if it had been freshly oiled just for me, but I stood there holding my duffel bag and I was unable to step forward. The air nipped at my face tamely; at least in comparison to the freeze in my heart. I was really going to do this. I was going to run away. But was I going to escape or was I hopping out of the frying pan to some infinitely worse nightmare?

Suddenly the street was no longer muted, but obnoxiously loud. It screamed in my face and battered my skull, making the thoughts I had built up so carefully over the past month scatter. "Where are you going to go?" it screamed. "You're going to die, you're going to die!" Amidst the roar I tried to listen for something, anything, from within the house to tell me that my mother was coming. A creak of a door or a footstep or even my name, but there was only the roar of her new boyfriend's snore and the screams of the dying trees in front of me.

Finally tears began to trail down my cheeks, and all at once I couldn't hear anything at all; not even the wind making the dark branches click against each other. I could feel the gold leaking out of me, tear by tear. I could feel the gray arms of the house slowly wrapping about my shoulders with bruised and bloody knuckles. I could hear it whisper to me, and the whispering hurt my ears and made me cringe and cry more. Instinctively I began to cry through choked breaths.

Nature's first green is gold, her hardest hue to hold. Her early leaf's a flower, but only so an hour. Then leaf subsides to leaf. So Eden sank to grief. So dawn goes down to day, nothing gold can stay.

"I can't stay," I said aloud. "Nothing gold can stay. I can't stay!" The wind now rustled through my shortened hair like a sweet caress, and I crossed the threshold of my mother's door and shut it swiftly behind me. I took out my cell and dialed a number.

"Hello? Hey, it's Anne. Yeah, I left. I told you I was serious. Yeah, I got the pills, you addict. Come pick me up. I'll meet you at the station. The train station, not the bus station, dumbass. How the hell am I supposed to get to Portland on a bus? Yeah, well, I dated an idiot, just get over here."

It was 5:10 when I left my life behind and walked towards the end of the street. It was 5:50 when I reached the Baja Fresh down the city street. It was 6:00 when the sun began to rise, painting the city in a thousand shades of pink and red and sweet honey gold. I watched as my ride slid into the empty parking lot, and I took a deep breath and stepped into my future.